Nina is a retired primary school teacher of nearly 30 years' experience. She was diagnosed with MS about three years ago. She is no longer able to walk but is able to use a tricycle which she uses nearly every day, accompanied by her able-bodied husband. Nina has three children, four grandchildren and a dog. She has always been fascinated by Science Fiction and the wonders of magic.

Dedicated to my lovely family.
To Jonathan, my husband of 40 years. (Thank you.)
To my children, Matthew, Naomi and Bekki. To their partners, Liz, Christian and Nick. To our grandchildren, Zack, Amelia, Sebastian and Tamsin. Not forgetting our children Katie and Luke, who live on, but not in this life.

Nina Pearce

WILLIAM AND THE CLYEOPHOS

AUSTIN MACAULEY PUBLISHERS™

LONDON ∗ CAMBRIDGE ∗ NEW YORK ∗ SHARJAH

A CIP catalogue record for this title is available from the British Library.

ISBN 9781528994842 (Paperback)
ISBN 9781528994859 (ePub e-book)

www.austinmacauley.com

First Published (2019)
Austin Macauley Publishers Ltd
25 Canada Square
Canary Wharf
London
E14 5LQ

Chapter 1

The moon glowed like a crystal orb in the darkening sky. The night felt heavy, there was definitely a storm approaching. William knew that he had to find shelter, and soon. Almost as if it had heard him, there was a distant rumble of thunder. He shivered even though it was not cold. The rain began to splatter on his clothes leaving wet smudges on him. He began to run, stumbling over the tree roots on the forest floor. "Damn and blast!" he complained as he fell over. Slowly, he stood up and brushed the leaves from his damp clothing. *Where to now?* he thought, as he tried to find his bearings.

Nothing, he thought, as he looked around, *there is no shelter here. That's all I need – to be here in the middle of nowhere, in an awful storm, with nothing to give me any protection.*

A sudden noise woke William from his self-pitying reverie. It was the bark of a nearby fox. Something had disturbed it and it had barked a warning. William hid behind a tree, trying to pinpoint the new sound – footsteps squelching through the undergrowth.

"There's nothing here!" shouted a rough voice. "Only a fool would be out in this weather."

"I saw William heading this way, he must be here."

"In this weather, are you totally barking? William will be tucked in somewhere warm by now; not out in this weather. Let's leave now and come back tomorrow when we may find what he was looking for."

William heard the second voice grumbling as the two moved away through the undergrowth, back to civilisation.

By now, William's eyes had adjusted to the dark and he could see shapes nearby, somewhere dry he might find to rest, while he thought things out and decided his next move. A sudden flash of lightning lit up the area around him; he could now see clearly a rough round shelter which he might be able to use. The wind and rain whisked around him, further flashes of lightning and crashes of thunder shook him as he made his way to, what he hoped was, safety.

Strangely, there was clean, fresh-smelling dry straw on the floor. William didn't think anything of it as he gratefully sank into the inviting warmth of the hay carpet. He was soon sound asleep; not even the thunderstorm, which raged around him, woke him as he slept the dreamless sleep of the overtired.

Chapter 2

William awoke to the smell of warm, fresh bread, and coffee. He lay still for a moment breathing in the comforting smell. Suddenly, he remembered where he was and sat up with a surprised yell.

During the night, someone had put a cover over him. Dazed, he shouted, "Who's there?"

"Why, hello, I'm glad to see you're awake at last; it's nearly lunchtime already."

"Who are you and what are you doing here?" William asked, sounding even less confident than he felt.

"First things first, come and have something to eat and drink," she replied. "It's not poisoned!" she added, seeing him look doubtfully at the tray then at the person holding it. She was a very tall, slender woman of indeterminate age, with a sheaf of black hair, which had a glistening stripe of silver down the centre and seemed to have a life of its own.

"Who are you?" he repeated.

The woman did not reply straight away, but pushed the tray of welcome food and drink towards him. William reluctantly took it from her and began to eat chunks of the warm bread and drink the steaming mug of strong, hot, welcoming coffee.

"My name is Esmerelda and you are in my home," she told him. "I saw you hiding from those louts in the woods last night."

William remembered. He also knew that they would be back again this morning. "I… I have to go," he stuttered. "They will come back. I was looking for something. They will trash this place and make me give it to them when I have found it."

Esmerelda laughed softly, "No, they won't. They won't even find this place. Anyway, I have cast a spell of confusion around here so they will get lost and disorientated."

William laughed derisively. But then he heard stomping coming closer. "Quick, I have to go. Perhaps I can lead them away from here so that they will leave you alone."

Esmerelda put a finger to her lips and beckoned William to follow her to the door of the cottage, which she flung open. William could clearly see Scrag and Scar-face searching the undergrowth, swearing as they were scratched by the brambles. "Where is he?" whined Scrag. "He and the thing he was looking for must be here somewhere."

"I told you he'd have gone home last night and will come back today, now that goddamn awful storm is over. Let's look in those bushes over there."

Scrag and Scar-face moved cautiously towards the bushes, away from the cottage William was in, in full view of the two thugs, but they did not seem to notice he was there!

He looked back at Esmerelda and could see she was grinning at him. She went back into the cottage, closing the door behind her. "Now," she said, "I think we need to talk."

William felt he could trust her as he hadn't been able to trust anyone for a long time. He started slowly, but as his confidence and trust in Esmerelda grew, he became expansive and soon began to tell her what had happened and why Scrag and Scar-face were looking for him.

Chapter 3

The daylight dimmed as the evening began to drift its tentacles over the land. William realised that he was famished as he hadn't eaten or drunk anything since the welcome breakfast hours ago. He looked at Esmerelda who was sitting with her legs underneath her, rather like a superior cat from one of the Egyptian stories which William had so liked to read when he was younger and enjoyed looking at the pictures of the cats in the books. Esmerelda suddenly noticed the time and rushed out to another room and was soon back with some hot food and drink. William had never before seen the food he was given. The salad, at least he thought it was a salad, seemed very unusual, with a strong taste of herby, garlicky wild mushroom. Not that he was sure of what it was. It wasn't unpleasant just different. His grandmother would have been amazed at the sight of him tucking in greedily anything which wasn't pasta-based or hadn't an accompaniment of chips!

"This is nice," he mumbled with his mouth full of – something. "What is it?"

"Senturally mixed with drionium and tophuratum, served in a slice of manciorcis bread."

William looked confused. "I don't normally try anything new but I must be hungry, and this is delicious!"

Esmerelda looked pleased and blushed slightly as she handed him more food. There was silence, only broken by the sound of William's devouring of the unusual feast.

"It's no good!" moaned a familiar voice. "We haven't found that brat William or the thing he was looking for."

"Hmm…" replied Scar-face, "perhaps he already has it and is now offering it for sale to the highest bidder."

"You know, I'm sure I can feel someone watching us. Come out, William. We know you're in here somewhere!"

The two boys stood still looking all around, including straight at the cottage where William and Esmerelda stood watching the two of them.

"They can't see us, can they?" asked William uncertainly.

"No, of course not. My hiding spells are renowned in the area; no one can break the spell if I don't want them to."

The two boys began slashing at the undergrowth, taunting and jeering at each other as their sticks destroyed bushes and small saplings. "That's enough now, Scrag, we'll go back home and see what Dionysus wants us to do next."

The noise of the boys' destructive rampaging gradually decreased and then stopped as they moved out of sight.

Chapter 4

William let out a long sigh of relief. "Phew! That could have been nasty. I wonder what they are going to do now?"

Esmerelda paused for a few moments and turned to look at him. Then without speaking, she turned and busied herself in the kitchen. The silence grew heavy as William waited for her to speak. Finally she came through the door wearing a jacket, thick walking boots and carrying a torch of some sort. "Come on then," she said, "we'd better find where the meteorite landed and recover the capsule, before anyone else starts looking for it."

William looked shocked. He didn't remember telling Esmerelda about the capsule, just that there had been something which seemed to fall out of the sky by the waste ground.

"How do you know what I'm looking for? I never told you what it was."

"Oh, for goodness sake, we haven't time for this. Come on!"

William looked mutinous and glowered at her.

"I'm a Clyeophis, a creature of magic and space travel," she explained patiently. "Oh, I see from your look that you haven't heard of us. That meteorite, or spacecraft, was delivering provisions and other things to me, but it hit a satellite and crashed not far from here. That's what I have been waiting for."

William looked even more confused. "You're a Kily whatsit? What's that and why are you here?"

Esmerelda didn't speak for what seemed like ages, but at last she continued, "We have always been here, not me but some of my kind. We're the guardians of your planet. There are guardians on many different worlds throughout the galaxy."

"How come I've never heard of you or your kind and no one else I know has either?" William retorted rather rudely, but, fortunately for him, Esmerelda didn't seem to notice.

She handed him his jacket and went through the door, obviously meaning for him to follow. William did as was expected of him and could only see Esmerelda's black hair flowing behind her as she sped through the forest. For someone of her age, she was very spritely on her feet. William was out of breath by the time he caught up with her. "Where are we going?" he gasped.

"The ship came down over there, I think. The capsule should be somewhere nearby," she replied.

"Stop what you're doing!" came an abrasive voice of an old man. "There is something here I need. Scrag and Scar-face, get off your lazy backsides and bring young William to me."

The two, grumbling all the while, grabbed hold of William roughly and dragged him over to the old man, who was leaning on his stick. "Well, where is it?"

William could tell that this man wasn't someone to be brushed off, so he said, "I don't know what it is or where, but I think it is somewhere close by."

"Well, you had better start looking, and quickly. I haven't got all day."

William looked around, but could see nothing out of the ordinary, not even a crater where a meteorite could have crashed. Then he looked around and realised to his horror that Esmerelda was nowhere to be seen. His only friend had perhaps disappeared, or perhaps she was never there, and he'd made her up.

"Where is Esmerelda?" he asked, though, he was sure he knew the answer.

"What do you mean? You are on your own, as usual, you loser!" Scar-face jeered. "We found just you stumbling about, as you normally are."

William thought for a moment, but had no idea what had happened. Why was he looking for something that didn't seem to be there and where was Esmerelda?

Chapter 5

William thought back to when he first became involved. It all started with a scrap of paper handed to him when he was playing in a local football match. He was in goal and one of the few spectators handed him the ball and the note. He shoved it into his pocket and forgot about it. His team lost the game by 14 goals. He had spent most of it fetching the ball out of the back of the net, trying to cope with the unpleasant taunts from his teammates and the delighted cheers from the opposition. It didn't bother him whether his mum and dad had married before he was born, that didn't make any difference to his playing ability. He really was the best goalie in his team and he did make quite spectacular saves on occasions. Not today though, he was all fingers and thumbs, he couldn't even catch a cold!

"Oi you, hurry up, what are you faffing about with? Dionysus wants the treasure found now!" Scarface shoved his face into William's, the spittle running down his brutish face as he spoke. William stood up, looked around and shrugged.

"I don't think it's here," he said quietly. "I'm not even sure what it looks like."

"What do you mean? Of course it must be here, why else would you bother to break a nail if there was nothing to find?"

"It's alright," said the deep voice of Dionysus, "we'll take him with us. He'll change his tune once he's had a chance to cool off in the chiller."

Scrag and Scar-face grabbed William roughly and dragged him off to a beat-up van where they shoved him inside, slammed the door, got into the front and drove off noisily.

William couldn't see anything through the journey. He was jostled about as the van drove down unmade roads. He felt rather queasy when, at last, the van pulled up and William was unceremoniously shoved into a damp, dark and a rather unpleasant smelling cellar. It smelt of weeks-old socks and William gagged as the door was bolted behind him.

"You will stay there until you come to your senses," promised Scar-face. "We'll see what you're like in a few hours." The two left William and he soon heard the van splutter as it drove away.

What was he to do now? He thought back to how he had got into this mess. It was that scrap of paper. William had forgotten about it until he was on his own. He took it out of his pocket and unfolded it. He looked at it for a long time without understanding. The paper seemed to have a series of meaningless squiggles in a curious circular pattern, but as he stared, he gradually began to make sense of it. *Treasure,* he read, *valuable treasure worth finding. Look in the old quarry.* William pondered the note and memorised the drawings. Suddenly, the unpleasant faces of Scrag and Scar-face came into view.

"What have we got here?" exclaimed Scar-face as Scrag tore the paper out of William's hands. "Err... it's a nipper's drawing. Did you do this on your own?" he jeered

"Give it back! It's private!" shouted William.

"Ooooh, it's private. It must be worth something. I think we'll keep this. Let's find out what Dionysus wants us to do with it," Scar-face continued, and they laughed as they pushed William over and left him there as they rushed off.

Chapter 6

William had been plagued by odd thoughts, separate words which kept coming into his mind, no matter what he was doing. *Capsule,* was the word that floated into his mind while he was watching TV one afternoon. He decided, or the decision stamped itself into his brain, that he absolutely had to go and find it that evening. Which was why he had been out in that storm, William, who enjoyed his comfort and was no fan of getting wet or being out in the dark or being on his own.

He had no idea now what he was going to do. He tried the door, but it was well and truly bolted.

William tried shouting, but of course there was no one there.

"Hello, William," came the voice of Esmerelda. "Would you like some help?"

"Yes, please. What are you doing here and why did you vanish when Dionysus got me?" William heard the scraping of the bolt as the door opened and he was able to leave the filthy smelling cellar.

"We can't stay here," answered Esmerelda. "Dionysus is on his way to make you get the capsule for him."

"Hang on," said William. "If Dionysus knows about the capsule, why can't he get it himself or get those two goons to do it for him?"

Esmerelda looked sadly at William. "Only you can get it. Dionysus knows that he cannot find or use the capsule, only you can."

William looked confused. "Why?" he said at last. "I'm no one special. Anyone should be able to get it. Why does it have to be me?"

Esmerelda sighed and continued, "You have been chosen by the Clyeophenes to do wonderful things in your future. You were chosen at birth. Haven't you ever wondered why bad things seem to miss you?"

William snorted, "Sprgh! What a load of rubbish! Nothing ever goes right for me. Unlucky is my middle name." He began to sound like he was whining. *Well, it is true*, he thought, *my life has been one long line of troubles*. Then he thought, *what about that time when I was running across the road and that motorbike just missed knocking me over?*

As he continued to think, he remembered other things, other times. The car crash that killed his parents and sisters, but he wasn't even there. He was furious because he had to travel with his grandparents as there was no room in his parents' car. He felt it was so unfair. That was until they came across the wreckage of the cars with the ambulance and police cars around. "Joyriders" they had been told. His family never stood a chance. It was strange, now he thought about it, how he witnessed many near misses, but never anything which would hurt him. That's why he had the reputation of being rather soft, always on the edge of trouble, but never in it.

Esmerelda led William out of the ramshackle building and suddenly, they were back in her cottage by the forest. William was totally confused. He had no idea how they had got there. He looked at Esmerelda shocked and a little frightened.

"Don't worry, it's just a little bit of simple magic, nothing too difficult," she reassured him. "I'm here to help you. It was written down in the past that I would one day have to help you."

"I don't want your help," he told her. "I just want to be left on my own, in peace."

"Do you really think that I wanted to do this and wait for the time I had to help you?" Esmerelda sounded cross. William began to feel rather ashamed of his behaviour.

"I'm sorry," he said. "I don't know why I'm here or what I'm supposed to do, but I'm glad you're the one helping me."

"Well, the first thing we have to do is work out where this capsule is and rescue it," she continued. William looked around properly for once and noticed that the cottage was a lot nicer than it had appeared when he first found it. For a start, there were more rooms, and instead of straw on the floor, it looked rather grand with a wooden floor. There was even furniture and William was sure that the shelter he had found last night was basically just somewhere to keep out the wind and rain.

"It's dark now," Esmerelda continued. "We could go out now, or we could wait until first light and look for it then."

William thought about it and realised he hadn't even told his grandparents where he was. "I'd better phone home. Do I tell them about you?"

Esmerelda smiled. "Yes, of course. They actually know me, you know. Just tell them you're with Esmerelda, they will be fine with that."

William took his mobile out of his pocket and phoned his family. Luckily, when they heard who he was with, they were delighted.

"I'm so glad you've met at last. Esmerelda told us you would meet her when the time was right," exclaimed his grandmother delightedly.

"Give her our love," added his grandfather. "Tell her she's welcome here anytime."

Chapter 7

Esmerelda and William talked long into the night as they planned what he was going to do the next morning. At last, with the plan sorted, William was shown to a proper bedroom, with clean sheets and an amazing duvet cover full of spaceships, planets and stars. Once again, he quickly fell asleep with no dreams to disturb him and it seemed like only a few minutes had passed before Esmerelda was knocking on the door and bringing him a welcome mug of tea. "It's nearly 5 o'clock and it will be light soon. There is toast in the kitchen. Eat it quickly, and then we must go."

William groaned. He really wasn't a morning person. He grumbled as he drank his tea, got dressed, ate a bit of toast and followed Esmerelda into the forest. Was it his imagination, or had Esmerelda's cottage grown in the night? He was sure that when he first spotted it, it was barely a shelter. Now a well-tended garden greeted him outside of the rather up-market cottage, complete with wisteria around the front door. Esmerelda had already left the garden and was now striding purposely through the forest. Once again, he marvelled at how fast she could move. He was panting with effort and was slightly sweaty when he caught up with her.

"Now, where?" he panted. "I can't see a crater or a hole anywhere."

"What's that over there then?" Esmerelda pointed to a dip in the undergrowth. It looked very recent, possibly made only last night, but that was impossible as he had already been looking for two days. How could it have only just happened?

William went over to the crater and began looking.

"You're going to have to do better than that. You will have to dig a bit, I think," Esmerelda said brightly.

William muttered something rude under his breath and started moving the fresh earth from the path where he was standing. "There's something here," he shouted. "I am sure it's the spacecraft."

"Try and uncover it a bit more," shouted Esmerelda excitedly, "then you can get the capsule." William carried on moving the earth using a spade mysteriously provided by Esmerelda. Soon, the object was uncovered and William could see something, something small and silvery, glittering brightly out of the uncovered hole.

"There it is! Quick, grab it before William gets it!" shouted Dionysus. Once again, when William looked around, Esmerelda was nowhere to be seen. Scar-face pushed William out of the way as he went to the hole and then looked up, with a more confused than his usual moronic look. "There's nothing here," he said. "William must have got it already."

William could also see that the capsule had gone. Scrag grabbed him and spun him around to face Dionysus. "Well, my boy," he said pleasantly, "where has it gone? It was here a minute ago."

"I don't know. I saw it, and then you turned up and it just vanished," William told him.

This wasn't completely true. Yes, it was no longer in the hole, but William could feel something pressing against his shirt. *It must be the capsule!* Suddenly,

William gasped as the capsule actually entered his body. "Ow!" he exclaimed. "What on earth was that?"

Everything went black and William could feel himself falling to the ground as he became unconscious and blood began staining his jacket red. He was aware that Dionysus shouted to the two goons that they had to leave now because someone was coming, then he knew no more.

Chapter 8

William came to, to the hustle and bustle of people all around him. Paramedics were checking his vital signs, and then he was lifted onto a stretcher and carried to a waiting ambulance.

"Did you see the truck that hit you?" asked a concerned policeman. He opened his eyes and saw to his amazement that he was now in the middle of a large town, full of people going about their daily lives, and a little way down the side street was a large Grey truck, which was on its side.

"No," he said. "I don't remember anything until I woke up here."

"That truck came out of nowhere very quickly down the hill. William and I were just going to get a cup of coffee. I'm his aunt," Esmerelda added as she got into the ambulance as well. "How is the driver?"

A tall, sweating man rushed up to the policeman. "That's my truck! I only left it for a moment while I paid for my fuel. When I came out, it was rolling down the hill. I'm sure I put the brakes on." He had obviously run down the hill, so was unable to prevent it from ploughing into William walking along the street.

William hadn't remembered that happening. He looked at Esmerelda, but she put a finger to her lips. He was aware of a sharp pain in his chest. Looking down at his clothes, he could see they were covered in blood.

How did that happen? Had he really been hit by the truck or had the capsule done that when it entered his body?

"Don't try to move," said a paramedic, as William tried unsuccessfully to get off the stretcher. "We're going to get you looked at, at the hospital. I'm sure you have broken some bones. After all, the truck that hit you is now on its side."

The paramedics shut the doors of the ambulance and it set off, sirens wailing, to the local hospital. When they arrived, William was rushed straight into an examination room where there were doctors and nurses waiting to sort him out.

"Well," the doctor said at last, "we can patch you up, but you won't be running about for a few weeks."

William's leg was broken in two places. He had cuts to his chest, where he was sure the capsule had entered his body. He thought he could feel it near his heart, but now there was a dressing covering the front of his chest. Esmerelda pushed William to the front of the hospital where he was given an appointment at the fracture clinic the next day. Once they were out of the hospital, William wondered how they were going to get back to Esmerelda's cottage as she pushed him to the corner of the next street.

"We're here, thank goodness. I don't think I could have pushed you much further," Esmerelda panted as she pushed William gratefully through the gate and into the cottage.

"How on earth did we get back here?" asked William. "There is no hospital near here; so what did you do to get us back here?"

"I told you," Esmerelda said slowly as if William were slightly slow-witted. "I'm a Clyeophos, a creature of magic and space travel. Work it out, William. Think!"

So William thought and realised that Esmerelda had obviously used magic to get them back here; magic, to make herself disappear when Dionysus turned up; magic, to find William when he was in that cellar and magic, when the capsule turned up and went into his body. In fact, Esmerelda had obviously done loads of magic and that's why the cottage had changed so much. Where had she come from? He now wondered. William was rather worried and scared now, he had to admit. He turned and looked at Esmerelda. She looked at him, slightly bemused at what he was thinking. "I thought that to do magic you had to have a wand which you waved around while you recited an incantation."

"Oh," exclaimed Esmerelda rather sharply, "I suppose you were expecting the pointy hat, warts and a black cat as well!"

William felt rather foolish, but he really wanted to know exactly how she had done all those things. He was suddenly overcome with a weariness he hadn't ever felt before. At once, Esmerelda was very concerned and put him to bed where he was once again sound asleep, without any dreams, or nightmares.

Chapter 9

William awoke to the sound of an engine which rumbled in a satisfyingly throaty way. He was no longer in the cottage but in a craft of some description. Esmerelda was busying herself at the controls. "Ah, William, you're awake at last," she announced. "You definitely know how to sleep through anything."

William moved the covers of his bed and was able to sit up though, not move his legs very easily.

Esmerelda introduced him to the other people on the ship; he still wasn't sure what type of craft it was! Xenion waved as he was introduced and Gapheren pointed to the last member of the crew, who was called Zettes. William worked out that Xenion and Gapheren were probably male and Zettes was a young woman, not much older that he was. "It's nice to meet you," he said at last, "but where are we going and why?"

Gapheren replied, as he didn't appear to be doing anything at that moment, "Esmerelda called us in the night and we decided to come and get you straight away as it isn't safe for you on your planet anymore, especially as the capsule has accepted you as its host."

"But I don't want it," complained William. "I just want to be left alone to get on with my life."

"You are aboard the spacecraft Superiority. It's the most advanced ship in this solar system and beyond," Zettes said rather proudly. "It is no longer safe for you to remain on Earth now that you have the capsule. There are many enemies who want it, or you, or both."

"But why?" asked William. "What does it do, apart from hurt, that is?"

At that moment, William gasped as the capsule moved again in his chest. He didn't think he would be able to survive this much longer.

"Don't worry," Esmerelda reassured William. "The capsule will let you know what it is going to do for you."

William grunted, not convinced that this thing was anything more than an awful pain, which had already caused him far more trouble than it was worth.

"Sit back and enjoy the view," Esmerelda told him. "We're not going to arrive at the space station for at least 24 Earth hours. Perhaps you will know what the capsule can do by then."

William looked out of a viewing port. He could see Earth! He had only seen photographs of it before. He hadn't realised quite how beautiful it was. He absorbed the view and was surprised to notice that Earth was turning. It didn't seem very fast, but Great Britain had already moved out of sight and he was looking at the vast continent of Africa, he thought. He was sure that he could make out deserts there, but when he told Zettes, she told him it was very unlikely. As William looked out of the porthole at the view, more places became visible. That was definitely an ocean and he was sure there were ships on it and in the sky below, he could see aeroplanes!

William pondered the things he saw but said nothing for the fear of being laughed at. He noticed Esmerelda looking at him closely and realised that she at least knew what was happening to him. The capsule was beginning to work in William's mind. What else was it going to do? At least it had stopped hurting now. He even felt comfortable sitting on this strange craft absorbing everything around him.

Esmerelda brought in some welcome food and drink. This time, William was too hungry to question what he was being given and he and the crew tucked into the feast with great enjoyment. He was sure that his drink contained some kind of alcohol which made him feel very happy and contented. A pressing need to visit the loo made him ask Xenion where he could go and he was shown to a compartment, not unlike what you get on a train, but much sweeter smelling. Feeling relieved and replete, William returned to his seat and continued to gaze at the way Earth was unfolding beneath him. William suddenly realised that his leg was no longer broken! As he felt along it, the plaster had gone and his leg seemed whole again. He tentatively stretched and moved it, there was no pain, just his ordinary leg – *The capsule*, William decided

He gradually fell asleep again as he was lulled by the motion of Superiority and the humming of its engines.

Chapter 10

An alarm sounding in the control room quickly roused William from his sleep. There were loud, angry voices coming from the bridge. He looked through the viewing port, but was shocked that he could no longer see Earth or even the moon from any of the ports on the craft.

"Where are we and what is happening?" William asked

Everyone seemed too busy to answer him but shouted to and at each other as they rushed around pressing buttons on the many different consoles, which were blinking different coloured lights and making the room seem far too bright and extremely busy.

"How did they find us?" asked Gapheren.

"I'm sure we left no traces or even clues as to where we were going," Xenion swore, or at least that's what William thought he was doing as he sounded furious, but William didn't know or understand what the sounds he made meant.

Esmerelda came over to where William was standing. "We have been found by the Sandriones. Dionysus is one of them. He still thinks he can get the capsule from you. He doesn't know that it has become part of you now."

"Sandriones," Esmerelda told William, "is a rather unpleasant race of people who usually stole things they needed, or thought they needed, from any creatures on any world. They didn't have magic, but that didn't stop them trying to cut the magic out of others for their own use."

"It doesn't work like that," said Esmerelda sadly. "My mother was murdered by them, when a gang of seven tried to get her to give them her magic. When she refused, they tried to cut it out of her. It killed her and they still didn't have any magic."

"Why didn't your mum make herself disappear like you did?" asked William. He was rather scared by what Esmerelda had just told him. He didn't want any Sandriones cutting the capsule out of him.

"She believed that when she told them she couldn't give them her magic they would just leave her alone. She had no idea that they were going to try to get it by any means. I was asleep in my bedroom at the time, and I didn't even hear her die. I was only a youngster; it has taken a long time for me to get over what they did to her."

William and Esmerelda were quiet as the rest of the crew continued to try and escape the Sandriones. William could now see the black spacecraft as it got nearer to them.

"That might just be enough to get us out of trouble," Esmerelda announced to the rest of the crew, and William. "I am going to try and cast a spell of invisibility around this craft so the Sandriones won't know where we've gone, or whether we were here in the first place."

William watched intently as Esmerelda began to make shapes in the air with her arms and nod her head in time to an unheard rhythm. She shouted one word in a strange language and they all waited to see if it worked.

Chapter 11

Bang! It was the noise of a missile heading towards them. It exploded as it hit a small piece of space debris. The Sandriones began circling the area but didn't seem to notice that the Superiority was still there. Zettes gave the order and the ship continued on its way towards the space station, leaving the Sandriones still circling and firing the occasional rocket at an invisible prey, which had now moved away. Esmerelda sat back in the chair and gave a sigh of relief. "Well, that will keep them occupied for a bit while they look for us in the wrong place."

The crew was quieter now as they busied themselves with the business of continuing with their journey. William thought about the capsule and tried to see whether what it had shown him of the Earth was real or a dream. He became aware of the capsule in his chest and could hear what the four crew members were thinking. He shook his head, not sure whether this was part of what the capsule could do.

William, said a clear voice inside his head, *just nod if you can hear me.* William nodded, wondering who was speaking inside his head.

This is Xenion, the voice in his head continued. *We will be arriving at the space station soon. Try and say something by thinking the words and not saying anything out loud.*

William thought hard and tried to think the name Xenion. He looked up at him and could see that he had successfully said his name in his head.

Good, continued Xenion. *It's useful to be able to think conversations when you want to communicate with an individual.*

William could see that no one else was aware that he was having a conversation with Xenion. *This is cool!* he thought. He looked over at him and could see Xenion smiling at him. Esmerelda came over to him and he heard her voice in his head as well.

Ah, I see you have discovered something the capsule can do for you, she said to William in his head. *Remember to look at and think about the person you want to have thoughts with; otherwise no one will know what you're thinking.*

William thought about Esmerelda and looked at her as he sent the thought, *Thank you.*

He now realised that the capsule had shown him two, or possibly three, things he could do with it. Seeing far away things very clearly, healing broken bones and telepathy. He wondered what else he would be able to do.

He jumped as a voice shouted out from the bridge, "The space station is coming into view; everyone needs to be ready as we land."

William was shocked at how loud the voice was, so he thought to Esmerelda, *That was loud!* She grinned at him and quickly took her place at the controls. He looked out of the viewport and as he concentrated, the space station became very clear. He could see another craft with people –no, that was not right – *creatures*, he thought, *Clyeophenes. How did I know that?* he wondered.

Chapter 12

Once the spacecraft had docked, Xenion, Zettes, Gapheren and Esmerelda busied about the craft turning equipment off and putting things away. It seemed amazing to William that they had just flown all the way from Earth and had a battle with the Sandriones. The spacecraft looked unused and possibly as new as when the crew first stepped aboard. Esmerelda spoke to William in his mind again, *We are all going to meet the high council now. Try to always tell the truth and answer politely when you are asked a question.*

William nodded, to show he understood the instruction, and followed Esmerelda down the steps of the craft into the waiting space station.

"Welcome to Station One, we are honoured to have you here." At that, a band of some description began playing. William assumed that what they were playing was music, though, it didn't sound anything like what he was used to. As he continued to listen, however, he became aware of the different sounds which made up the music. He began to appreciate that this group of musicians was rather really good. He was sure that this was also from the capsule, an understanding of another world's music.

William was disappointed when the band finished playing, he was rather enjoying himself. He followed the crew into another room where there was a huge table.

Esmerelda gestured for William to sit at one of the chairs and then sat next to him. The other members of the crew sat at the other chairs, with the important being at the head of the table followed by the rest of the high council. The being began by asking the crew how their mission had gone. Zettes explained what they had done and told of how the Sandriones had attacked them, which was why Esmerelda had performed a vanishing spell to make them disappear and left the enemy going around in circles, trying to find them.

"I'm glad this space station is also hidden," the being declared, "but I don't think they will have given up yet. Knowing the Sandriones as I do, they will be trying to find a way to get to us. We must be on our guard at all times."

William shivered as he thought about the Sandriones still searching and then trying to cut out the capsule from his chest when they found him. However, he brightened up considerably when huge plates of food were brought into the room, carried by several small creatures wearing identical, but extremely colourful, costumes.

Make sure you thank them for bringing you food, instructed Esmerelda in William's mind. William didn't have to be told because the food looked amazing. It seemed to contain many colours and a lot of different shapes. The effect was striking and, even though William was extremely fussy, he was anxious to try all the different foodstuffs. He realised that he was also very hungry; it had been a long time since the last meal on the ship. William looked round at Esmerelda and tried to copy what she was doing with the food. He was pleased that his choice made a very attractive arrangement on his plate. William waited until everyone had a selection of food on their plates. Looking at Esmerelda, William lifted his fork to take a bite out of the food on his plate.

When the being at the head of the table took a bite, so did William, and he was pleasantly surprised to note that it was once again the best thing he had ever tasted in his life. The drink made William feel incredibly relaxed and happy. He noticed that all of the diners seemed to feel the same way.

When at last the feast was over, the being, *Gan Jephus,* Esmerelda thought to William. *He is the leader of this space station.*

"Right," he said, "now to business."

William was aware that every head had turned to face him as they waited to hear what the plan for his future was.

Chapter 13

"Our top priorities are to prevent any attack by the Sandriones at all costs and to protect young William. I understand that the capsule has already accepted him as host and has begun to show what it can do for him," announced Gan Jephus.

William was slightly bemused by all this. What the capsule had shown him so far were no more than pretty cool party tricks, he wasn't sure how they would help him in the future. The capsule moved in his chest and a thought came to his mind, *Wait, there will be lots more I can do for you.* He rubbed his chest because of the pain the capsule caused him as it moved. He was sure, actually, that the pain was decreasing, no more than a slight ache now. No, he was now just aware that it had moved when the words came into his head. *I wish*, he thought, *that there was another way the capsule could let me know it wanted to say something, without pain.*

Ok, came the thought, *your right thumb will twitch.* At that, William's right thumb began to twitch and he waited to see what it would say to him.

Look at Gan Jephus, came the thought. So William looked at him and became aware that Gan Jephus was incredibly old, even though he looked no older than middle-aged. He had seen a lot of suffering in his life, including when Esmerelda's mum had been murdered.

William, came the thought in his head. William looked round and could see Esmerelda staring at him. He looked at her and knew that she was part of Gan Jephus' family. This must be something else the capsule does, see into a person and know where they came from and who was in their family. *Concentrate on what Gan Jephus is saying; don't get side-tracked,* she thought to him. At once, William looked at Gan Jephus and became aware that he had been asked a question. He looked blankly at Jephus, who helpfully repeated his question, "What would you like us to do for you?" He was asked.

"I… don't know… this has all been a bit of a shock really," William replied. "I don't like the thought of the Sandriones trying to cut the capsule out of me and I would like to speak to my grandparents, they might be a bit worried as I haven't been home for a few days and I only spoke to them once." William hadn't realised that he was, in fact, missing his grandparents. After all, they were the only family he had now.

Gan Jephus waved at a big screen William hadn't realised was there. Soon, the images of his grandparents could be seen, followed by their voices. "William," said his grandma, "how are you? Where are you? When are you coming back?" He could see that his grandparents looked worried, so he smiled reassuringly at them. "I'm fine," he told them. "Esmerelda is looking out for me. It's quite amazing what I've seen and where I've been."

William looked at Esmerelda who continued, "Yes, we have seen some great sights and he is behaving very well. You would be amazed at the different foods he is now trying and enjoying." She continued, "This is surely a once-in-lifetime experience. I must get him to finish writing you a postcard, or we will be back home before it reaches you. We have taken loads of pictures which we will get printed for you."

William's grandparents beamed at her and at William, clearly satisfied by what she told them of their travels.

"Take care then," his granddad said, "try not to get into any trouble while you're gone." William laughed. *Typical!* he thought. *They always think something will happen to me.* The screen flickered and then went off.

Chapter 14

Gan Jephus continued, "I can see that the capsule is beginning to work in you and you are becoming aware of some of what it can do."

William nodded, he was sure that the capsule still had more to show him. Right on cue his right thumb twitched. Esmerelda looked up as she noticed William's thumb moving.

Look at that glass over there, the capsule thought in his mind. William looked. *Point at it and think that you'd like a drink of water. Concentrate.* William looked at the glass and pointed to it, he thought about having a drink of water. The glass merely wobbled a bit and the jug of water nearby feebly splashed a tiny amount of liquid, which didn't even leave the jug.

This is hopeless, groaned William in his head. *That was rather pathetic!*

Don't give up, came the thought from Esmerelda, *have another go.* William tried again. This time, he concentrated so hard, beads of sweat broke out on his forehead. The jug moved towards the glass and then lifted, gradually tipping over as the glass began to fill with water.

Stop! thought William, as the glass became full. Then he moved his arm and the now-full glass came towards him and settled on the table with a small clunk and a splash, as it slightly spilled over the edge.

"Oh, well done!" Gan Jephus said, clapping his hands in delight. "That was brilliant for a first effort."

William picked up the glass and took a drink of wonderfully cool and refreshing water.

What next? he wondered. Gan Jephus continued speaking as he outlined the measures they would take for the space station and the reinforcements from their home planet which would be needed to ensure that the Sandriones would fail in their attempts to find William and try to make him give them the capsule. Esmerelda noticed that William was beginning to flag as the leader continued his speech. She gestured to the council and Gan Jephus immediately stopped speaking. The small creatures came in and took William to a room, where he was shown a very comfortable bed which he sank into gratefully and was once again asleep in seconds.

William awoke feeling very refreshed and rested. He looked at his watch, but of course, it was showing Earth time and he had no idea how long he had been asleep, or what time it was now. There was a sound at his door.

"William," came the voice of Esmerelda, "are you awake?" William jumped out of bed and went to the door. He pressed a button and it opened smoothly. Esmerelda handed him a change of clothes and pointed to where there was somewhere he could have a shower and freshen up.

"How long have I been asleep?" he asked.

"Oh, four cycles, I mean two days," she answered. "I think that the magic you did rather drained you, so you needed sleep to recover. When you're ready, I will get you some food and drink." Esmerelda left the room, leaving William to get himself cleaned up and dressed. The clothes he was given to put on were very different to what he was used to. There were underclothes, then a type of jumpsuit which did up by using a type of invisible Velcro. When he was ready, the door opened and William went out to be met by Esmerelda who took him to another room where there were many different types of food, including, William noticed happily, bowls of chips and pasta!

Chapter 15

William tucked heartily into his breakfast. He decided to try the strange and unusual foods as well as a bowl of his favourite tuna pasta, though, the dish which contained something he was sure was wriggling, he left well alone and just scrutinised other unusual dishes before trying them. He was rather pleased to discover that he liked those he tried even though he hadn't a clue what they were, perhaps it was better he didn't know! Other Clyeophenes came and tucked in. After everyone seemed to have eaten enough, the same, small brightly coloured beings rushed in and cleared the plates, bowls, and other debris created by the diners. When the other diners left the room leaving William on his own, he decided to explore the space station. No one had told him what he could and couldn't do, so taking his chance he followed some of the Clyeophenes into a rather impressive looking lobby. William noticed openings which looked worth an investigation, so being the person he was, he opened one of the doors and went through.

There were portholes he could look out of, so he focussed on a spacecraft leaving the station. William's right thumb began to twitch and he could see right into the craft as if there was no hull covering it! *Cool,* thought William. *I wonder where they are going.* The thought came into his mind that this ship was making a return journey to Clyeophos, Esmerelda's home planet.

William, came a thought into his head, *I need to show you around the space station. If you wander off on your own, you may well get lost and might even end up on another spacecraft!*

William thought, *OK, I'm sorry, I didn't know what I could do. Where are you?*

Think! came the thought back to him. William thought, and in his mind, he could see Esmerelda sitting in a room waiting for him, but he didn't know how to get there.

Concentrate on me, Esmerelda thought. So William did and suddenly found himself in front of her.

"That was weird!" he said aloud. "I haven't a clue how I did that, or did you do it?" he asked uncertainly.

"No, it was all you. The powers you have got from the capsule are beginning to manifest themselves strongly in you," Esmerelda replied with a grin.

Esmerelda showed William around the station. He was particularly impressed by the room which looked like a nursery, full of things growing in, what he supposed were, pots.

William looked carefully to see if he could recognise anything that he had already eaten but perhaps the plants, he supposed they were, hadn't fully grown yet. He thought he recognised the label on one of the plants. It was Senturally; he had tried that at Esmerelda's cottage. At the end of the room was another door which Esmerelda went through, expecting William to follow, which he did as he was finding the whole experience incredibly interesting, though a little scary, he had to admit. This room was rather dark and Esmerelda didn't try to make it any lighter. Along one wall was a huge screen and William could see displayed on it a large yellow planet. *Clyeophos*, he decided.

Chapter 16

"Yes, William, this is Clyeophos, my home planet," announced Esmerelda proudly. "It is the most beautiful place I have ever lived in."

William looked at it carefully. He could see what Esmerelda meant; it really was a lovely planet. He would love to visit it. He looked at Esmerelda enquiringly.

"Would you like to go there?" she asked.

"Oh yes, please," answered William eagerly.

"It might be a good idea to go soon, just in case the Sandriones find their way to the space station."

"But don't they know you come from Clyeophos?" William asked.

"Yes, but we are much better protected there than we are here in the middle of space," she continued. William wasn't sure how they could prevent Dionysus and his goons getting to him, but he decided to trust Esmerelda and do what she suggested.

"When are we going?" he enquired.

"Soon," came the reply. "We are just waiting for Superiority to be repaired after the encounter with the Sandriones, and then we will go."

William hoped that Xenion, Gapheren and Zettes would be the ones taking them back to Clyeophos, but he didn't think he could ask Esmerelda, so he continued to look carefully at the image of the planet on the big screen. His thumb began to twitch, which William realised, meant that the capsule was going to show him something, or perhaps speak to him, or both.

Look at the top right quadrant of the planet, it said in his head. William looked and as he did so, the quadrant became larger and more detailed.

Wow, he thought, *that's cool.* He continued to look intently at the enlarged image on the screen.

It's not an image, it's real, came the capsule's thought. *You are now able to see that part of the planet and what is going on there. Look harder.*

So William looked harder, and as he did so, he began to see buildings and the people inside them. That must be Esmerelda's house, he decided. Looking at Esmerelda, he was aware that she could see what he was looking at as well.

He looked at her and thought, *Is that where we are going?*

Yes, came the reply, *I didn't know that you had already begun to see places as they are, no matter how far away we are. You should try to see your home on Earth and see if you can contact your grandparents that way.*

William nodded, though he really just wanted to take in what he was seeing on the screen. Clyeophos really was beautiful. It knocked spots off Earth, it was so clean. For a start, there didn't seem to be any pollution about either. William didn't know how he knew that, but he was sure it was true.

Your home, came the thought in William's head. *OK,* he sighed and began to think of his home. The big screen on the wall changed. Earth was displayed and as William concentrated, England, his county, his village and then his house came into sharp focus. He saw his grandparents in the living room, drinking cups of tea and chatting to a neighbour who had popped round for a chat.

He looked round at Esmerelda, who nodded, "Yes, you can see them, talk to them."

William coughed and then said a little embarrassed, "Er… hello, it's me, William."

"What are you doing on our telly?" his grandmother asked.

"I don't really know, Esmerelda told me to speak to you."

"Oh, for goodness sake, it's a video call from our ship. There is a satellite link to your telly. Anyone would think it was magic!" Esmerelda complained, as William still looked slightly confused.

Chapter 17

William suddenly felt rather homesick. It didn't matter that he had been dismissive of his home and family; they were his, their shortfalls and all. He missed his bedroom with the old-fashioned wallpaper. His granddad had built his bed so that it fitted the wall. It was slightly bigger than a normal bed and they'd had to get a mattress specially made. "Don't you dare spill anything on the mattress. You won't get another one." He had been warned. His wardrobe was rather unique as well. He could walk into it; his football kits hung carefully on the hangers, he was able to pick the right one to wear depending on which team he was playing for or supporting that day.

Outside, the garden was overgrown, except for his grandma's herb garden, which had many scented herbs growing. Of course, William had always refused to taste anything his grandma had grown because it made him comfortably difficult. He was sure, however, that she occasionally slipped things into his meals to see if he noticed! William was surprised at how much he missed his home and especially his gramps. They were the only family he had left. His mum had no relatives and his dad only had his parents. There were no cousins or aunts and uncles in the picture. William wondered how his grandparents really felt about him not being there.

As if reading his mind, his granddad spoke to William, "We're really proud of you, you know, but we can't help missing you. Make sure you keep in contact with us. We got your postcard today, but it is great seeing you on the telly."

"Have a great time," added his grandma. "Tell us all about it when you get back."

Both his grandparents beamed at him and for the first time in a long while William realised that they actually cared about him. It came as a bit of a shock as he had felt for some time that no one was on his side or even cared about him. He was sure that the only person who cared about him was called William. He had his own issues, so was no help to him at all, he sighed.

William realised that he had been behaving rather badly for a long time, like a typical teenager he supposed: grumpy, surly and on occasions, downright rude and unpleasant to his family. He vowed to would change that, when he got back – if he got back. William smiled warmly at his grandparents and was gratified to see their surprised, but delighted faces, looking back at him.

"Love you loads," William said earnestly. "I promise that when I get back we must go on holiday together, wherever you want," he added as he remembered the last argument he had with them, when he told them he would rather eat his own feet than go on any holiday with them. He blushed slightly at the memory, but his grandparents were nodding happily with his mention of a holiday.

"Yes, we could go fishing in France again. You did like that, didn't you?"

"As long as you're there, anywhere will be great!" William finished and wiped his eyes as he noticed they had become damp. *Must be pollen about*, he decided.

The image of his grandparents, their home and Earth faded and William turned to look at Esmerelda.

"Well done, William," she said. "That will have dispelled any worries they might have been having about you. Bed, I think, as we have to leave this station tomorrow."

William yawned, he hadn't realised how tired he had become.

Chapter 18

William thought about his bed and then found himself standing by it! He gratefully sank under the covers after removing his clothes and was quickly asleep again. This time, however, his sleep was plagued by dreams, which he didn't understand and couldn't remember when he woke up. He was just aware of an uneasy feeling, which wouldn't go away, and the memory of them was there on the tip of his tongue. William woke, sometime later, feeling refreshed except for the thoughts just out of reach. He showered, cleaned his teeth (his grandma would be pleased!) and then got dressed. Thinking about breakfast, he pictured the room where it had been and found himself standing next to Esmerelda. She smiled, and then gave him a plate. William loaded it with the things Esmerelda had put on hers. There was something he was sure he'd hate, so he tentatively took a tiny bite. Yes, it was disgusting! Still, at least he had tried it. William noticed Esmerelda grinning at him as he moved the unwanted food to the edge of his plate.

Yes, she thought to him, *that does take quite a bit of getting used to; it's actually rather nice when mixed with soolyworms!*

William snorted; he was never going to try those disgustingly wriggly things!

They are a vegetable. They wiggle because of the way they are cooked, Esmerelda continued.

William picked up one of the soolyworms with his fork. It wriggled and almost fell back onto the dish. William could have sworn that it grinned at him! He quickly put it back and continued with the food he was sure he would like.

When everyone had finished, Esmerelda stood up and addressed Gan Jephus and the high council.

"Thank you," she began, "for your wonderful hospitality, but I think that William needs to be taken to Clyeophos where they are much better equipped to prevent the Sandriones getting anywhere near him."

"When will you leave?" asked Gan Jephus.

"In one cycle," replied Esmerelda. "We will take the crew of Superiority with us; it has all we need for the journey home."

"I'm sorry I didn't have longer to get to know you, William," said Gan Jephus. "If you ever want to pay us a visit, do come back. The station will always be available to you."

William shook hands with all the council members, then he, the crew and Esmerelda, began to make their way back to the spacecraft. There was the silence of the crew busying themselves with the preparations to leave. William knew instinctively that he needed to keep out of the way, so he sat in a seat and looked through the porthole as other ships came into the space station.

"Ready to leave?" came a strange, metallic voice through the loud speakers. Superiority powered up its engines and very slowly moved out of the space station.

"Next stop," announced Gapheren, "home!"

There was a cheer from Zettes and Xenion. They were obviously keen to go back to Clyeophos.

Chapter 19

The ship sped through the dark sky. There were many stars in the sky, which William knew from his science lessons, were actually suns in different galaxies. There was no idle chatter from the crew; they just got on with their different tasks, efficiently. William wondered how long the journey would take. His right thumb began to twitch and the capsule spoke into his mind, *We will be arriving in about three cycles, or nearly a day. Think about the blind on the porthole and try to make it go down.*

William thought and looked at the blind on the porthole. For a while nothing happened, and then the blind wobbled a bit, but didn't drop down. William panted with the effort.

Concentrate, came the thought. *Magic is never easy. You have to think really carefully and imagine the blind doing what you want it to.*

So William looked at the blind and imagined it dropping down the window. As he looked, it began to slowly unwind and drop down the porthole. He looked at Esmerelda to see if she had noticed and at once, the blind flew back up into its holder.

You must concentrate all the time when you use magic, came the annoyed thought from the capsule. William concentrated and the blind once again dropped, this time completely covering the porthole.

Make sure you tell the blind to stay so that it doesn't fly back up, came the thought from the capsule.

William looked at the blind and thought, *Stay!* The blind stayed where it was, covering the porthole. He let out a huge sigh of relief. *That was difficult,* he thought. *I don't think I could do that every day.*

"Don't worry," said Esmerelda. "It gets easier the more you do it."

William didn't think he wanted it to get easier. He was happier not doing magic if it was going to be this difficult all the time.

"Oh, look!" said Esmerelda with a note of pride in her voice. "I can see Clyeophos." William looked, but couldn't distinguish between the different stars and planets.

"There it is, behind our moon."

William stared at where she was pointing, perhaps that speck was Clyeophos. It was a bit like that game he used to play with his sisters, trying to be the first one to see the sea, when they were going on holiday. William always won that game, though he wasn't always sure that it really was the sea or conveniently placed clouds. Anyway, his family knew that looking for that tantalising glimpse of the sea kept him quiet for hours. Even after the sea had been spotted, he tried to work out whether the tide was in or out and if the sea was calm. If so, they could all rush down to the quay and let the dinghies out of the boathouse for a quick sail to make sure they could remember what to do and have a race to the harbour. William gave himself a little shake; he hadn't thought about his three sisters for a long time. He suddenly realised that he missed them. It wasn't their fault they were all killed in the car crash which also took his parents. William continued to gaze at the small planet, he was pleased to note that Esmerelda smiled at him.

"We will be there soon," she said.

Chapter 20

A loud voice sounded through the ship's speakers, "Warning! Warning! You must identify yourself or prepare to be annihilated."

"We are the spacecraft Superiority. We are returning home and have a passenger, William who has been accepted by a capsule. The Sandriones are looking for him. We ask for your protection."

"Welcome friends, we invite you to accept our hospitality. We have spotted the Sandriones on our long distance trackers. We didn't know what they were looking for, but our defences are strong and we are ready for them," continued the voice from the speakers.

Zettes turned round and looked at William, "Well, it looks like the Sandriones are on their way here. It seems we left not a moment too soon."

William was relieved that the crew didn't seem very bothered by this news, though, he was concerned. What would happen if they managed to get hold of him? He continued to worry. Perhaps that was what his dreams were about the other day, that sense of unease, just on the tip of his tongue, but with no idea of what he was worrying about. At that, his right thumb began to twitch.

You are much more powerful now, came the thought from the capsule. *Try and make yourself invisible.*

How? thought William.

Think about being unseen. Try to picture where you are, but without you being there, came the thought from the capsule.

So William thought. He imagined the cockpit without him being there, just a space where he was sitting. Nothing happened; he was still very much there. William groaned; he was never going to be able to disappear. Esmerelda came and sat next to him and asked him what he was trying to do. He told her what the capsule had asked him to do but had been unable to make anything of him invisible. Esmerelda thought for a minute and then said, "I always try to imagine myself in my favourite place, at home, in my kitchen."

"But how do you stop yourself travelling there?" he asked, wondering what his favourite place might be.

"You must keep focussed on where you are, so that your body goes, but your soul stays where you are."

William thought that still seemed very difficult. No, downright impossible! He didn't even know he had a soul. His favourite place came into view in his mind, ah, the boathouse on holiday. He pictured himself there, whilst still being on the ship.

Well done, William, came the voice of Esmerelda. *Look at your hands.*

William looked down at his hands, but they weren't there! He stared at the rest of him, but there was no sign of him. Was he a ghost?

OK, came the thought of the capsule, *you have done it, now come back from your favourite place.*

William slowly un-faded and solidified back on the bridge of the ship.

"You're back now," said Esmerelda. "How do you feel?"

William thought, *That was a bit weird!* He said, "I'm not sure I want to do that too often."

"I expect you're a bit tired now," she continued. "I'm rather surprised the capsule wanted you to do that so soon." Esmerelda sounded rather grumpy and William was surprised and touched by her concern for him.

"I don't really mind, at least I know what to do and it might be useful someday," William grinned.

"Just don't use it for unhelpful reasons. Spying on your friends only leads to trouble in the long run."

William wasn't too sure what Esmerelda meant by that remark. He could think of lots of useful, if not very kind, ways of using that ability. In fact, he was quite keen to try it out on other crew members, perhaps even Esmerelda herself.

Chapter 21

Suddenly, there was action from the crew.

"We're coming into land soon," shouted Gapheren. The crew rushed about, putting loose things away and William was shown how to put his seat belt on. He didn't know what landing was like on a spacecraft, but he looked at Esmerelda and tried to copy what she was doing. The landing seemed incredibly smooth, Superiority glided down with Zettes and Xenion operating the controls so that as William looked through the porthole, he could see many different creatures lined up waiting to welcome them.

William removed his seat belt and stood up when Esmerelda did. They followed the crew off the ship and into an amazingly huge and brightly coloured area. He was surprised by the opulence of it but now realised that Clyeophos must be quite a wealthy planet.

Yes, thought Esmerelda into William's mind, *we are wealthy. Our scientists have been able to develop things which creatures on other worlds are willing to pay vast amounts to get. The wealth is fairly distributed, so no one has to go without.*

What about crime? thought William. *Surely some people will always want more?*

No, came the reply from Esmerelda, *there is no crime. People are happy because they have everything they need. Don't forget that we can always magic other things we might want.*

William wasn't totally convinced by this, he was sure people like Scrag and Scar-face would want something extra. He looked more closely at the people in the crowd. They did seem happy, but surely someone, somewhere would be unhappy with their lot? William wasn't able to continue his thoughts about this, as yet again, a band started to play and he was captivated, once more, by the sheer complexity of the music. It was like nothing he had ever heard before. He didn't know anything about music, but he knew he liked this. In fact, it was better than his current favourite band. William allowed himself to become lost in the music. He closed his eyes and began to sway. Esmerelda tapped him gently on the shoulder. "Come back, William. You were lost in the music, but we do have things to do."

William shook himself and followed Esmerelda as she walked towards a type of car. Well, it had seats but no wheels. William wasn't quite sure how it would move. He sat beside Esmerelda and waited to see what was going to happen. He didn't have long to wait. One of the small colourful beings got into the car and asked cheerfully, "Where are we going?"

"Home," replied Esmerelda. With that, the craft began to lift and then sped off. William had no idea where home was, but he was determined to enjoy the ride and perhaps look for signs that not everyone was happy on Clyeophos.

The craft went through different areas, all spotless and wealthy looking. As hard as William tried to look, he didn't see anything which looked poorer than anywhere else on the planet. Creatures stopped what they were doing and waved as the craft went by. *This is too good to be true,* thought William.

No, came the thought from Esmerelda, *everyone is truly happy here; it's the best planet in our galaxy.*

"Why did you come to Earth then?" William said rather petulantly. "If it is so good here, why leave? Earth is not exactly a perfect place to live on, you can get mugged, or worse, anywhere."

"William," sighed Esmerelda, "you do realise that crimes don't happen all the time on Earth? Many people are happy, if not as wealthy as they'd like to be."

William grunted. He was not sure about that, the newspapers were always full of disasters and dreadful crimes committed against ordinary people.

"How many people do you actually know who have been murdered?" asked Esmerelda.

"Well, none actually, but I heard that there are places near home that you don't visit after dark," William finished; sure that life on Earth really was not great.

"Clyeophenes are guardians, and some of us have been chosen to look after different inhabited planets like Earth. Oh, look, we're here!" She finished excitedly.

Chapter 22

The craft drew up to a low building which, like the other buildings William had seen, looked amazing. Freshly painted, and no hint of rubbish or a quick tidy-up either.

Perhaps, thought William, *Clyeophenes really are a happy people. No,* he continued, *that's just a pipe dream, it can't be real.* Esmerelda quickly got out of the Shween, she told him and into the waiting arms of her family. William remembered that her mother had been murdered by the Sandriones when she was younger. She introduced him to them. Her father, rather stooped and somewhat withered, her brothers and their partners and children. *Quite a brood,* thought William to himself, as he was not sure what Esmerelda would think to hear her family being called a brood!

He was shown into a splendid room, where there was a magnificent dining table laden with food and drink. William knew what to expect now, so he sat down and when other family members began loading their plates with food, he copied them, trying to take things he knew he'd like. A cup of amber liquid was offered to him and Esmerelda announced that William, as the guest, should make a toast and drink the first drink. William felt very awkward and shy, he didn't know what to say! He had never made a toast before in his life and didn't know what to do. He looked at Esmerelda and thought, *Help me!*

Don't worry, I will help you. Raise your glass and tell my family about why you're here, she thought back to him, and smiling encouragingly William stood with his glass in his hand.

"Thank you," he began. "The Sandriones want to take the capsule away from me. It went into my chest back on Earth and the Sandriones have been trying to get it back ever since. They even followed me to the space station after Esmerelda got the spacecraft Superiority to rescue us and take us there. I don't really understand why you are helping me, especially Esmerelda, who was helping me at home, but thank you and I ask you to raise your glasses to drink a toast to Esmerelda, her family and all the Clyeophenes for their protection," William finished and sat down. Everyone drank a toast and the meal continued. Esmerelda beamed at William.

"Well done," she said. "That was lovely."

William felt a bit happier now that was out of the way and looked around at the other members of Esmerelda's family. He wondered what they really felt about opening up their home to him, not even someone from the same planet, someone who needed their protection and who probably had brought danger with him! Esmerelda's dad seemed happy to have William there, but he supposed Esmerelda probably didn't go home a great deal anymore, so he was happy for anyone to bring Esmerelda home. Her brothers too chattered away to each other and to Esmerelda, they even tried to include William in their conversation, but as he knew nothing about Clyeophos or the latest styles or culture, he was unable to say very much, so just listened carefully to the conversations all around him.

Chapter 23

William was amazed at how respectful Esmerelda and her brothers were to their father. William didn't do much more than grunt at his gramps these days. He felt rather ashamed (again) about this and resolved to behave much better, if he ever saw them again. He became aware suddenly that someone had asked him a question; he shook himself and looked around to see who had spoken to him.

"Ah, William," said Esmerelda's dad. "What would you like to do with your time here?"

"Well," replied William slowly as he continued to think about what he wanted to do, "I would really like to visit different parts of Clyeophos and meet lots of new people."

Esmerelda's dad nodded solemnly, "I thought you might. We're actually quite boring as a race; the beauty is in the area. There are lots of different places to explore." He continued, "I would like to see something of Ezzy before she takes you away again."

William smiled. He couldn't imagine being that important to anyone. He agreed that he would visit different families in the area and ask someone to show him around.

The meal finished, William was invited to explore the area around Esmerelda's home.

"It never gets dark here," one of Esmerelda's brothers said. "We have two suns and four moons." William hadn't noticed that, so he went outside to have a look. He could see the moons, which seemed to be arranged in a long line. The suns were trickier to distinguish. "The sun we go round is the one on the left; the other one is further away. It has its own planets going round it." William could see that now, the warmth from the first sun was on his face whilst the other one gave more light. He realised that there were no dark hiding places and wondered how people slept here. No wonder his watch didn't tell the correct time, it must be confusing trying to work out what the time was, there didn't seem to be any way to distinguish day from night even. He didn't even seem to have a shadow! *Weird,* he thought.

Yes, came a thought back from the capsule, *that is one of the reasons people are genuinely happy here. No dark spots to cloud people's minds or feelings.* William still didn't totally buy into that, but he was finding it hard to come up with proof of any bad behaviour or antisocial leanings from anywhere. He wondered what the moons were called. The thought came back from the capsule– *from left to right, blue moon, green moon, yellow moon and big moon.* William looked and he now noticed that the moons were different shades of colours. The big moon, however, was huge. He continued to stare at the moons and then noticed the vegetation. He had never seen anything like it before, even at the Eden Project or Kew Gardens, where he had, in spite of himself, enjoyed visiting the biomes. There were plants of many different hues, tiny plants and much bigger ones. William, who had been expecting green leaves, saw that the plants had many colours, even on the same one. Not a green leaf to be seen.

William shook himself; the effect was rather noisy and busy, not unpleasant just unusual.

Chapter 24

William tried to hide himself in one of the nearby bushes. It was big enough to hide in and had an unfamiliar perfume, not cloying rather pleasant in fact. Whilst he was hiding, a small bird flew onto one of the branches and began to sing a melodious song, like the nightingales at home. William remained entranced by the song and then became aware of voices. He thought it came from Esmerelda's brothers who were talking intently to each other.

"Do you think the Sandriones will come here for William?" one of them said.

"Bound to. They want that capsule back, and even if they can't use it once it has been removed from him, no one else will be able to either."

"Oh, hello William, what are you doing?" the first brother exclaimed, pleased to have found him.

"Er... I was listening to a bird which landed in the bush," William explained lamely.

"It's impossible to hide here, the birds always let us know if something is where it shouldn't be," the second brother Nibort explained. "Hide and seek usually only lasts minutes before everyone has been found."

"Am I in danger?" asked William to the brother who had mentioned the Sandriones.

"You could be," replied Nibort truthfully. "It seems that the Sandriones have found a way to beat our security, they could be here soon."

"Can't you hide the planet?" asked William desperately. "Esmerelda hid her cottage back on Earth from Scrag and Scar-face. She also managed to hide Superiority when it was being attacked in space."

Esmerelda's brothers explained that whereas it was possible to hide a planet, it would only work if people didn't know where it was already. The Sandriones had attacked them several times in the past, so they knew where to go. They were also looking for him, and he wouldn't be hard to find in a group of Clyeophenes, as he looked nothing like any of them.

"What can I do then?" William asked. "I must leave here so that you're not at risk from the Sandriones."

"Too late," muttered Nibort. "You forget they came here before. Esmerelda's gift of magic is still quite rare, only given to those who will use it wisely for others and not selfishly."

"Why have I got it then?" William complained. "I didn't ask for it, nor do I want it. I wanted to be a famous football player."

"Huh. I've seen you playing," Esmerelda laughed, rather unkindly, William thought. He glared at her. Suddenly, a loud voice came booming out. "People of Clyeophos," it said, "we have come for the Earth boy William. Give him to us and we will leave you in peace. You have 2 cycles."

There was a loud explosion, which sent up a plume of smoke in the distance.

"That is just a warning, in case you think to hide him from us," the voice continued. "The next time there is an explosion people will be killed, unless we have William. Bring him to the spaceport."

William looked around wildly. What could he do?

Don't worry, came the thought from the capsule. *There is a way to save you and this planet.* The others also looked around wildly. Esmerelda came quietly to William and thought to him, *This is just the beginning. They won't let us go even if we do give you to them.*

"What do I do then? Surely there must be a way out of this mess. I wish I'd never come here and put you all in danger," William said desperately. At once, his right thumb twitched and he felt the capsule moving inside him. There was a loud siren. "Everyone on this planet has heard that. It is the defence signal. We must all go to the underground shelters. The Sandriones have never been there, so we will be hidden from them."

William could see a problem with that. What was to stop the Sandriones from blowing up the whole planet if they didn't find anyone? The capsule spoke in his mind, *You must let the Clyeophenes hide underground first. Then we will go and meet the Sandriones, once they are all safe.*

"Am I going to be like the sacrificial lamb?" he said at last.

No! came the thought, *I will always be with you, just trust me and you will be fine. Come on.*

Chapter 25

William thought about being at the spaceport. He looked up and saw slightly to his dismay that he was already there. The Sandriones were waiting for him.

"Kill him!" came the triumphant shout from Dionysus. At his signal, armed soldiers lifted their weapons and aimed them straight at William. *That's it then,* thought William. *I wish I could have seen my grandparents once more.* He wasn't sure why he wasn't panicking. He just seemed to be accepting his fate, knowing that once they had killed him and removed the capsule, they would set about destroying Clyeophos as punishment for trying to help him. William also wondered what the Sandriones would do once they discovered that they couldn't use the capsule. Would they punish Earth by destroying it and killing everyone living there? William waited for the final shot, and then he opened his eyes, wiped away his tears and saw that Dionysus and the Sandriones were not moving!

"What happened?" he asked. "Why haven't they killed me?"

"You sound disappointed," remarked Esmerelda, walking towards him. "I have stopped time around them. We must quickly decide now what we are going to do."

"Can't we just put them on their ship and send them home?" queried William.

"Possibly, as long as the time-stop holds. I'm not sure if I made it strong enough. Oh, I'm sure it will be OK. Come on."

Esmerelda strode over to the gunmen and quickly removed their weapons. She removed the power packs and threw them away. "Now they're harmless pieces of junk," she declared, looking at the pile of them on the ground.

William and Esmerelda carried the time-stopped Sandriones onto their ship.

"No need to make them comfortable," she declared. "Just dump them in the hold."

It was back-breaking work, moving 11 stiff Sandriones, but at last they finished. Esmerelda put the ship's controls to auto and they hurried off the ship as it began to power up.

"Well, I hope that's the last we see of them. I'm not sure where they will be going, but, hopefully by the time the time-stop ends they will be far away and not know how they got there and why."

William chuckled wryly. He hoped Esmerelda was right, but even if she wasn't, it should buy him more time.

Esmerelda stood quietly for a time. She was obviously listening to something. After what seemed a long, boring time, she turned to William and told him that the Sandriones' ship was still heading off into space at an incredible speed. "There is still no movement on the ship, so I suppose the time-stop must still be working. My grandfather did a time-stop once on some Lianstorums who were trying to steal from him and it didn't lift for five Earth years! By the time they realised what had happened to them, their whole planet had changed beyond belief. I think the Lianstorums found it hard to cope with, so they lived the rest of their lives as hermits, unable to face being a part of society. They were a very greedy race. They didn't trouble us again," she finished in a very satisfied sort of way.

Chapter 26

William wasn't sure what to make of this. It was another side to Esmerelda he wasn't quite sure he liked very much. *Better not get on the wrong side of her,* he thought to himself.

Hear, hear! thought back the capsule. *Just make sure you don't get her really annoyed.*

Hmm, thought William, *what is going to happen now? Am I going home?*

"That's up to you," announced Esmerelda. "Do you want to go home now?"

"What will happen if the Sandriones find me back on Earth?" he queried.

"Don't worry about that. At the very least, it could be years before they come round, and then they would have to remember why they were hunting you. Earth is not as easy to find as you think it might be. After all, you haven't even got a working space programme yet."

"You found us," said William grumpily.

"Yes, but we are creatures of magic and space travel. We found your planet long ago and have been trying to help ever since."

And now you have the magic from me, thought the capsule. *It is up to you whether you want Esmerelda to accompany you back to Earth or not.*

William thought about it and decided on the whole he'd rather have Esmerelda with him on Earth. After all, his grandparents liked her, and so did he, actually. Well, most of the time. Though, she did scare him quite a bit.

"How are we going to get back home?" asked William. "And, will you come with me?"

Esmerelda stopped pacing round and turned to face him. "We will use the spacecraft Superiority and transport by magic from your moon. We don't want anyone on Earth realising that a spacecraft has been there."

The time passed incredibly quickly as preparations were made to take Esmerelda and William back to Earth.

"What will the capsule do now? Do I still need it?" queried William

Of course you still need me! thought the capsule in his head. As if to make the point, it also gave him a sharp twinge in his chest.

"Ow!" yelled William. "Surely, that wasn't necessary. That really hurt."

William could have sworn that the capsule chuckled. *Sorry,* it thought to him, *I'll try not to do that again.*

Hmm, thought William, *whatever!*

"Come on, don't just stand there, we have got to move."

William shook himself, rubbed his chest and took the things Esmerelda gave to him. He helped load the ship, and after a long while they were ready to leave.

William was really keen to be on his way home and after some long and slightly tedious speeches from worthy people of Clyeophos, they were on their way.

The capsule asked William to do lots of magic on the way home. He was surprised to find it less taxing now to make things like the blinds go up and down, or pour himself a drink. He even remembered how to think himself somewhere on the ship, and then see himself instantly there.

"We're approaching the moon now," Esmerelda informed him. "I think I will let you try to relocate us there, somewhere near your back garden would be a good idea. Don't forget to concentrate on it and imagine yourself there."

William tried, but he was having problems remembering what his garden actually looked like. Then he remembered his grandma's herb garden. He concentrated with all his might. Slowly, the garden solidified in his mind, faintly at first, then clearly. Then he was standing in among the mint, there was a heady smell of it as he accidentally crushed some of the plants.

You forgot to include me and your things, came the plaintive thought from Esmerelda. William thought again and then Esmerelda and his things arrived in and near his grandma's herb garden.

"Quickly, get out of the herb garden, we need to go and see your grandparents," Esmerelda announced as the back door opened and out came his grandparents.

"William!" said his delighted grandpa. "You're back, at last. We're very pleased to see you both." Esmerelda quietly shoved a present into his hands which he gave to his grandma, who had followed his grandpa out of the house.

The next few hours were filled with a delicious meal and lots of conversation about William and Esmerelda's fictitious travels. William was amazed at how accomplished a liar Esmerelda actually was. Still, she did make their adventures sound amazing. In fact, part of William believed they were true.

What now? thought William to the capsule. *Are we safe now?*

Sort of, came back the reply. *There is no sighting of the Sandriones in the near or far distance, but they may be back someday. Until then, why not enjoy being a normal teenager for a bit?*

William looked at his grandparents and smiled. Being a normal teenager, that's what he had been doing with the grunts and zero conversation. Perhaps, he'd grown up a bit, past the surly teen. He hadn't really tried growing up yet, but why not, he could at last make up for the times he was a bit of a jerk to them, perhaps even enjoy school, or at least try to get back into the football team again.

William thought about the things he could do and without thinking, he got the jug of water and filled a glass with his mind. Looking up, he was aware that his grandparents were now sitting, staring at him with their mouths open.

Whoops! he thought. *I'd better try and explain my way out of that then!*

Esmeralda whispered a few words and both his grandparents fell back into their seats, asleep.

"Well," said Esmeralda. "I think I'd better stay with you to keep you out of trouble, at least for the time being. Don't worry about your grandparents, William, they will wake in a moment and no time will have passed for them. We will still be discussing our recent adventures."

William breathed a sigh of relief, things would be different for him now, but at least he had the capsule and Esmerelda to help him.

His grandparents awoke and carried on as if nothing had happened. *What an adventure,* he thought, *I hope things will get back to normal now, I wonder when my next football match is?*